Facing Fear

Abhaya Vidyā

Swamini Vimalananda

Central Chinmaya Mission Trust

•

First Edition - December 2014 - 3,000 copies
Reprint - October 2015 - 2,000 copies

•

Published by:
Chinmaya Prakashan
The Publications Division of
Central Chinmaya Mission Trust
Sandeepany Sadhanalaya
Saki Vihar Road, Powai, Mumbai 400072, India
Tel.: +91-22-2857 2367, 2857 5806
Fax: +91-22-2857 3065
Email: ccmtpublications@chinmayamission.com
Website: www.chinmayamission.com

•

Distribution Centre in USA:
Chinmaya Mission West
Publications Division
560 Bridgetown Pike, Langhorne, PA 19053, USA
Tel.: 1-888-CMW-READ, (215) 396-0390 Fax: (215) 396-9710
Email: publications@chinmayamission.org
Website: www.chinmayapublications.org

•

Designed by:
Chinmaya Kalpanam, Mumbai

•

Printed by:
Usha Multigraphics Pvt Ltd., Mumbai

•

Price: ₹ 65/-

•

ISBN: 978-81-7597-666-5

CTP

Content

Transliteration and Pronunciation Guide

In the book, Devanāgarī characters are transliterated according to the scheme adopted by the International Congress of Orientalists at Athens in 1912. In it one fixed pronunciation value is given to each letter; f, q, w, x and z are not called to use. According to this scheme:

Devanāgarī	Translit-eration	Sounds Like	Devanāgarī	Translit-eration	Sounds Like
अ	a	son	ढ्	ḍh	adhesive*
आ	ā	father	ण्	ṇ	under*
इ	i	different	त्	t	tabla
ई	ī	feel	थ्	th	thumb
उ	u	full	द्	d	this
ऊ	ū	boot	ध्	dh	Gandhi
ऋ	ṛ	rhythm*	न्	n	nose
ॠ	ṝ	**	प्	p	pen
ऌ	ḷ	**	फ्	ph	phantom*
ए	e	evade	ब्	b	boil
ऐ	ai	delight	भ्	bh	abhor
ओ	o	core	म्	m	mind
औ	au	now	य्	y	yes
क्	k	calm	र्	r	right
ख्	kh	khan	ल्	l	love
ग्	g	gate	व्	v	very
घ्	gh	ghost	श्	ś	shut
ङ्	ṅ	ankle*	ष्	ṣ	sugar
च्	c	chuckle	स्	s	simple
छ्	ch	witch*	ह्	h	happy
ज्	j	justice	ं	ṁ	improvise
झ्	jh	Jhansi	ः	ḥ	**
ञ्	ñ	banyan	क्ष्	kṣ	action
ट्	ṭ	tank	त्र्	tr	three*
ठ्	ṭh	**	ज्ञ्	jñ	gnosis
ड्	ḍ	dog	ऽ	'	a silent 'a'

* These letters don't have an exact English equivalent. An approximation is given here.

** These sounds cannot be approximated in English words.

भवानीशङ्करौ वन्दे श्रद्धाविश्वासरूपिणौ ।
याभ्यां विना न पश्यन्ति सिद्धाः स्वान्तस्थमीश्वरम् ॥

Salutations to Goddess Pārvatī and Lord Śiva who are the embodiment of faith (in the scriptures and the Guru) without which even the great Masters cannot realise the Lord seated in their own heart.

वन्दे बोधमयं नित्यं गुरुं शङ्कररूपिणम् ।
यमाश्रितो हि वक्रोऽपि चन्द्रः सर्वत्र वन्द्यते ॥

Salutations to Ādi Guru Lord Śiva, the embodiment of Knowledge, by whose refuge, the sickle-shaped and crescent moon also becomes worshipped everywhere.

नित्याय मुक्ताय शिवात्मकाय नव्याय भव्याय परात्पराय ।
शुद्धाय बुद्धाय निरञ्जनाय नमोऽस्तु ते सद्गुरुचिन्मयाय ॥

Salutations to Sadguru Śrī Chinmayananda who is ever liberated, the embodiment of Lord Śiva, ever new and glorious and the supreme, pure, untainted Consciousness.

Preface

I am by nature fearful. I have travelled alone with a knapsack on my back in some parts of the north and south of India for a period of six months in my pūrvāśrama. An elderly saint in Gangotri told me, 'I see fear in you. How come someone so young is travelling alone?' I realised then that right from childhood, I had learnt to face fear rather than back out. In fact, I was taught to face fear. As a child, I was scared of dark places. My father would say, 'Find out what is in the darkness that you are afraid of'. I would then venture into the darkness and overcome fear. This attitude of facing fear (has still not made me completely fearless) but has made me adventurous, hold my own in a man's world, accept the worst case scenario in any circumstance, unafraid of being unpopular (which I am!) and enjoy solitude. Also, I was very fortunate to be in the company of a truly fearless divine person in the form of Śrī Gurudev, Swami Chinmayananda. He reinforced my will to face fear and encouraged me to live in solitude.

The *Abhaya Vidyā* happened during one of my periods of solitude. I beg forgiveness of everyone for my audacity (dhṛṣṭatā) for having written it in the style of an Upaniṣad.

Upaniṣads are mantras revealed to Seers in their seat of meditation. They are not man-made and are sacred eternal Truths. I do not even dare to call myself a serious seeker, leave alone a Seer. I am grateful to all the great Seers for their revelations which inspired the style of *Abhaya Vidyā*. This is only because, during that period of solitude I was doing pārāyaṇa (reading) of the 108 Upaniṣads. Its influence was so strong that the words that emerged were in Sanskrit (of which I know very little), many words right out of the Upaniṣads and in the Upaniṣad style.

This is only and only a creation for my own reflection and satisfaction (svāntaḥ sukha). For more than twenty years I did not show it to anyone except Pūjya Gurujī who kindly corrected the Sanskrit. During the Dharma Sevak Course in 2009 at Ahmedabad, I spoke on it for first time. It was liked by all, I believe, because we all have many fears in us. This gave rise to the thought of putting it into a book form.

Preface

I am a student of Vedānta and Upaniṣads are the very essence of Vedānta. All thoughts in *Abhaya Vidyā* are culled out from the study of Vedānta. Many are the sentences directly quoted from various Vedānta texts.

Continuous prostrations and deepest gratitude to Pūjya Gurujī for the opportunity to write again and again.

This is an humble offering to Bhagavān Śiva, who is my very own Self – free from all fear. May He be pleased and bestow true fearlessness.

I thank Smt. Asmani, Bengaluru for the cover design and Śrī T.B. Thakur, Tarapur for sponsoring the first print of this book. They have both always been a great support to me. May Gurudev's blessings be with them always so that they continue with the good work.

All credit for the thoughts expressed goes to the Guru-paramparā. All shortcomings are due to my limitations.

Swamini Vimalananda
Śivarātri 2014

Vedānta Darśana
– An Introduction

It is important to understand a few basic principles of Vedānta. 'Veda' means to know or Knowledge. Vedas are eternal truths that govern the universe. They are not composed or invented. They are not even discoveries but are revelations. Ṛṣis (mantra draṣṭās) realised them either as mantras or knowledge in their seat of meditation. They taught them to their disciples who in turn meditated on them and passed them on to their disciples. They are also called Śrutis as they were heard by the disciples and passed on through the Guru-disciple-lineage (guru-śiṣya-paramparā). Thus the Vedas are not man-made (apauruṣeya).

Knowledge is eternal. It is neither created nor destroyed. It gets manifested with the thing created and becomes unmanifest with its destruction, like the law of gravity. Since the Vedas speak of eternal Truths, they are eternal (nitya and sanātana). The Hindu Dharma is therefore actually called Sanātana Dharma.

The Vedas were compiled by Śrī Veda Vyāsa into four volumes called the *Ṛg Veda, Yajur Veda, Sāma Veda* and the *Atharva Veda*. Each of us is born with three manufacturing defects. The first is the impurities of the mind (mala) like desires, anger, greed, jealousy ... the list is long! The second is the distractions of the mind (vikṣepa). O! the wandering of the mind and how difficult to catch it even for a moment. The third is the ignorance of our own true nature (avidyā āvaraṇa). We think we are a finite being whereas we are actually the infinite Truth! Each of the Vedas was therefore divided into three sections – Karma Kāṇḍa, Upāsanā Kāṇḍa and Jñāna Kāṇḍa. By practising the knowledge of the first two sections, we can get rid of the impurities and the distractions of the mind. The last section helps us to dispel ignorance. The first two sections give us knowledge of Dharma which ensures a harmonious life here, and a good life hereafter. The last section gives us knowledge of Brahman (Truth) which liberates us from the here and hereafter. The Jñāna Kāṇḍa is also called Vedānta or Upaniṣad.

Upaniṣad means 'near-down-sit' (upa + ni + ṣad). It is the knowledge we attain when we approach a Guru and sit near him (upa samīpe) with all humility and determination (niścayena). It is the knowledge of the infinite Truth (brahma-jñāna/ātma-jñāna) which exhausts the inherent tendencies (vāsanās) of lifetimes, dispels the ignorance and reveals our true nature.

In this world, there are two types of attainments. One is of the thing not yet attained (aprāptasya prāptiḥ). When a thing, person, state or status is away from us in time and space, we can attain it through right knowledge and right action, like travelling to a destination or becoming a CEO. However the Self/Truth is one with us, already attained, but appears to us unattained (as we keep looking for happiness outside) because of ignorance. The only way to attain it is through Self-knowledge. It is not attained by any number of good actions nor is it the result of meritorious action, as actions and their result are both finite, whereas the Self is infinite.

When the known object (prameya), the means of knowledge (pramāṇa) and the knower's mind (pramātā) are aligned, knowledge (pramā) takes place. When the book is in front of us, and our eyes are open and the mind is awake and available, we read these words and understand! In case of Self-knowledge, the Self (prameya) is always available, ever the same, night and day. Thank God! The Self cannot be perceived through our senses or conceived through our mind or logically inferred. The Upaniṣads are the only valid means of Self-knowledge.

Since the knowledge is extremely subtle, we need a Guru, who can teach us the right meaning of the scriptures. The best Guru is one who is well-versed in the scriptures (śrotriya) and well-established in the Truth (brahma niṣṭha). The second best is one who is well-versed in the scriptures as he can give us the right knowledge. Therefore the knowledge of the Upaniṣad or Vedānta given through the Guru is the valid means of Self-knowledge.

Knowledge somehow does not seem to arise even when taught by the Guru, several times, over years! This is because the third factor, the seeker's mind (pramātā) is not well prepared. The four-fold qualifications needed in the disciple are:

a. The ability to discriminate between the eternal and the ephemeral (nitya-anitya viveka)

b. Dispassion (vairāgya)

c. The six-fold wealth (ṣaṭ sampatti) – control of the senses (dama), control of the mind (śama), withdrawal from revelling (uparati), forbearance (titikṣā), faith (śraddhā) and absorption (samādhāna)

d. Desire for Liberation (mumukṣā)

Spoken differently the seeker's mind must be pure, concentrated and subtle.

a. **Purity (śuddhatā):** A mind free of desire, anger, greed, attachment, arrogance and jealousy is said to be pure. The pure mind has good intentions for all – even one's enemies, is naturally cheerful, loves all unconditionally and without inner motive. It is said that God bestows Knowledge on one who surrenders to Him totally with a pure mind.[1]

b. **Concentration (ekāgratā):** It is the ability to focus on a single thought or task to the exclusion of all else. This is most valuable for all students and seekers. But unfortunately nothing is done to cultivate it. It is easier for one with concentration to meditate on the Self and gain absorption (samādhi).

c. **Subtlety (sūkṣmatā):** It is the ability to see a thing 'as it is'. It is the insight into a subject which is holistic and deep. It is also referred to as the sāttvika intellect by which one knows what is right and wrong, what should be done or not done, and what is bondage and Liberation.[2] The Truth can be realised – known as It is – by one with a subtle and

[1] *dadāmi buddhi-yogaṁ taṁ yena mām-upayānti te.* – *Gītā* 10.10

[2] *pravṛttiṁ ca nivṛttiṁ ca kāryākārye bhayābhaye,*
bandhaṁ mokṣaṁ ca yā vetti buddhiḥ sā pārtha sāttvikī. – *Gītā* 18.30

concentrated intellect.[1] A subtle intellect is acquired by study of the scriptures, reflection and meditation.

The seeker who has all three – pure, concentrated and a subtle intellect – realises the Truth effortlessly and immediately.

The first step that a good shooter takes is to clean his gun and load it. He thereafter focuses the gun, steadies his hand and concentrates on the goal. He finally pulls the trigger and the bullet hits the target.

How does one realise the Truth? Vedānta recommends three sādhanās.

1. **External practices (bahiraṅga sādhanā):** The spiritual practices required to make the mind pure, concentrated and subtle or equipped with the four-fold qualifications is called bahiraṅga sādhanā. It includes performance of one's duties with right attitude, cultivating values, performing rituals and so on.

2. **Internal practices (antaraṅga sādhanā):** These include listening, reflection and meditation.

[1] *dṛśyate tvagryayā buddhyā sūkṣmayā sūkṣma–darśibhiḥ*
– *Kaṭhopaniṣad* 1.3.12

a. **Listening (śravaṇa):** It is not merely hearing the scriptures, but it is to ascertain the import of the scriptures or what the Guru or Vedānta conveys. It is to determine not what we understand of the Truth, but what the scriptures say is the Truth. When a well prepared seeker does śravaṇa, he realises the Truth.

b. **Reflection (manana):** The second step is only needed for those who do not realise as they listen. Reflection is not possible without right śravaṇa. Reflection is the churning that takes place in the mind of the seeker, between what the scriptures say is the Truth, and his own experience. Through this, his doubts get resolved and he finally comes to the same conclusion of the Truth, as conveyed by the scriptures. A seeker can realise the Truth by its very ascertainment.[1]

c. **Meditation:** The third step is needed only if realisation has not taken place through the first two steps. Only when śravaṇa and manana are done well that nididhyāsana becomes effective. Meditation is to own one's true nature again and again. Because of the habit of innumerable lifetimes, we automatically identify with the

[1] *tattva-niścaya-mātreṇa prājño bhavati nirvṛtaḥ*

body-mind-intellect. The constant practice 'I am the infinite Truth' removes this habitual error.

3. **Direct means (sākṣāt sādhanā):** Ignorance manifests in the mind as thoughts like, 'I am finite, I am the doer, I am born ... '. This can only be removed by the thought 'I am the infinite Truth'. Therefore, even though the Self/Truth is beyond the mind and the purview of thoughts, the 'mature thought of Knowledge' (paripakva akhaṇḍākāra vṛtti) is needed to remove the ignorance. Therefore the great importance for a well prepared mind. Atleast at the time when the knowledge-thought arises, the mind has to have the four-fold qualification. This can be attained by one's own effort blessed by the grace of God and Guru. The knowledge-thought removes the ignorance-thought and having served its purpose, disappears to reveal the Self/Truth. This is called Realisation/Self-knowledge/Liberation. Therefore Realisation is said to be spontaneous, effortless and immediate.

Ignorance once dispelled, never makes a comeback. Thank God! In fact, the wise man realises that he was never bound as the Self/Truth is ever liberated (nitya mukta).

1 Facing Fear

Abhaya Vidyā

This composition is based on the actual experience of a seeker when she was in solitude. It is written as related by her.

कदाचित् ह वै महाजलाशयमध्ये रमणीयैकान्तस्थाने द्वीपकुटीरे कश्चित् कृष्णसर्पः शिवम् आराध्य पूजास्थाने एव उपस्थितवान् आसीत्। तदा गुरुवरेण दीक्षिता काश्चित् साधिका शिवाराधनार्थं तत्र गता। सर्पं दृष्ट्वा अतीव भीता सा। तथैव च सर्पः। शिवं विस्मृत्य परस्परं दृष्टवन्तौ॥

तदा सा साधिका उवाच - किमर्थमहं भीता? मदात्मा सर्वभूतात्मा। त्वमपि मदात्मैव। मायामात्रमिदं सर्वं दृश्यम्। सर्पवृत्तिः भयं च सर्पोऽपि मिथ्यैव। शिवस्य भक्ताः बान्धवाः। त्वं मम बन्धुः। शिवभूषणः सन् मम आराधनार्हः। भयत्यागेन सुखिनौ भविष्यावः। अहिंसा व्रते सुनिष्ठिताहम्। मा भैष्ट। भो गच्छ। सुखी भव॥

kadācit ha vai mahājalāśayamadhye ramaṇīyaikāntasthāne dvīpakuṭīre kaścit kṛṣṇasarpaḥ śivam ārādhya pūjāsthāne eva upasthitavān āsīt, tadā guruvareṇa dīkṣitā kāścit sādhikā śivārādhanārthaṁ tatra gatā, sarpaṁ dṛṣṭvā atīva bhītā sā, tathaiva ca sarpaḥ, śivaṁ vismṛtya parasparaṁ dṛṣṭavantau.

tadā sā sādhikā uvāca – kimarthamahaṁ bhītā? madātmā sarvabhūtātmā, tvamapi madātmaiva, māyāmātramidaṁ sarvaṁ dṛśyam, sarpavṛttiḥ bhayaṁ ca sarpo'pi mithyaiva, śivasya bhaktāḥ bāndhavāḥ, tvaṁ mama bandhuḥ, śivabhūṣaṇaḥ san mama ārādhanārhaḥ, bhayatyāgena sukhinau bhaviṣyāvaḥ, ahiṁsā vrate suniṣṭhitāham, mā bhaiṣṭa, bho gaccha, sukhī bhava.

कदाचित् - Once upon a time; ह वै - indeed; महाजलाशयमध्ये - in the middle of a large lake; रमणीयैकान्तस्थाने - in a beautiful solitary place; द्वीपकुटीरे- in an island (where there was) a cottage; कश्चित् कृष्णसर्पः - one black snake; शिवम् आराध्य - having worshipped Lord Śiva; पूजास्थाने एव - amidst the altar only; उपस्थितवान् आसीत् - was seated; तदा - at that time; गुरुवरेण - by a Master; दीक्षिता - initiated; काश्चित् साधिका - one seeker; शिवाराधनार्थं - to worship Lord Śiva; तत्र गता - went there; सर्पं दृष्ट्वा - having seen the snake; अतीव भीता- very scared; सा - she (became); तथैव - so was; च - and; सर्पः - snake; शिवं विस्मृत्य - forgetting Lord Śiva; परस्परं - each other; दृष्टवन्तौ- saw

तदा सा - then she; साधिका- seeker; उवाच - said; किमर्थमहं - why I am; भीता - scared; मदात्मा - my Self; सर्वभूतात्मा - (is) the Self in all; त्वमपि - even you; मदात्मैव- are my Self; मायामात्रमिदं सर्वं - this is all an illusion; सर्पवृत्तिः - thought of the snake; भयं - fear; च - and; सर्पोऽपि - even the snake; मिथ्यैव - are false only; शिवस्य - of (Lord) Śiva; भक्ताः - devotees; बान्धवाः - relatives; त्वम् - you (are); मम - my; बन्धुः- relative; शिवभूषणः - ornament of Śiva; सन् - having been; मम - my; आराधनार्हः - (you are) worshipful; भयत्यागेन - by giving up fear; सुखिनौ भविष्यावः - we both will be happy; अहिंसा व्रते - in the vow of non-injury; सुनिष्ठिता - abide firmly; अहम् - I; मा भैष्ट - don't be afraid of me; भो गच्छ - now you leave; सुखी भव - be happy

Once upon a time, in the middle of a large lake, on a beautiful solitary island, there was a cottage. In that cottage, a snake, having worshipped Lord Śiva was seated in the midst of the altar. At that time, a seeker who was a disciple of a great Master, came to the prayer room to worship Lord Śiva. She was very scared when she saw the snake. So was the snake. Forgetting Lord Śiva, both of them stared at each other.

Remembering all that she had learnt, she said to the snake, 'Why am I scared? The Self in me is the Self in all. You too are my own Self. All that is experienced is, after all, an illusion. The fear, the thought of the snake and the snake are all part of the illusion and therefore false. Why should I be afraid of you? Also, the devotees of Śiva, belong to Śiva's family. As Śiva's family all are related to each other. You are thus, my relative. (So why should I fear you?) Besides, being the very ornament of Lord Śiva, you are worshipful to me, who considers everything associated with Śiva as worshipful. (So why should I fear you?) If we leave our mutual fear we will be happy. Also I abide firmly in the vow of non-injury. So do not be afraid of me. Please leave. Be happy.'

Creative thoughts take wings in nature. This little creation had a truly scenic setting. A tiny island in the middle of a vast crocodile infested lake, deep and dark, where lightning streaked and rain poured down in sheets. Snakes slithered and birds flittered. Scorpions were regularly avoided and leopards were occasionally sighted. Worldly cares were scared of the crocodiles and worldly fares could not ride the choppy waters. The elements were in their element and moments of beauty and peace stretched leisurely.

The mind was immersed in the worship of Śiva and in the thoughts of Vedānta. It was a dream solitude.

Great discoveries are uncovered in moments of silence and masterpieces spring out of masterly triggers. This simple piece was triggered by fear. I've seen plenty of snakes of different varieties and in sizes in āśramas where I've lived and in my solitude, both inside my residence and outside. But I've never seen one sitting snug in my altar! The unexpected encounter scared both of us.

Silence and solitude prompt us to find all solutions within. So even in this scared state I could stand back and talk to myself and the snake. Firstly, I was sure that what I was perceiving was not a snake vision on the rope – an example I've heard and spoken of hundreds of times in Vedānta lectures. Then I asked, 'But why am I scared?'

Have I not learnt that the Self in me is the Self in all. You are my own Self, then how can I be scared of you?

Have I not studied that the entire perceived and conceived world is an illusion that includes the snake, its perception and my fear of it. How can I be scared of an illusion?

Have I not chanted each day – 'God Śiva is my father, Goddess Pārvatī my mother, God's devotees are my relatives and God's creation my home?'[1] Snakes love Lord Śiva and are therefore His devotees and therefore are also my relatives. How can I be scared of those who are my own? Swami Ramatirtha was travelling to America for the first time. An American approached him as he stood on the deck of the ship and asked him if he had friends in America who would be taking care of him. Svāmījī said, 'Yes, I know you.' And that person did take care of him. Svāmījī could even look upon strangers as his own.

Have I not understood that anyone and anything associated with God is divine? Śrī Kṛṣṇa's flute is worshipped and so are the Guru's pādukās (sandals). Snakes are Lord Śiva's ornaments. I see them adorning His matted Locks, His neck, His ears and His arms, each day in the picture in my altar. How can I be scared of His divine ornaments?

---

[1] *mātā ca pārvatī devī pitā devo maheśvaraḥ,*
bāndhavāḥ śivabhaktāśca svadeśo bhuvana-trayaṁ.

I have vowed to live my life with as little harm to any other living being as possible. But if you are in a striking posture, how can I not be scared? So please do not strike. How then can I be scared when we both have decided not to harm each other? Please go your way, so we can both get along with our work.

At this point I would like to reflect a little, based on the book *Gift of Fear* by Gavin de Becker. I too agree that at the transactional level, fear is a God-given instinct or intuition which helps humans survive and that we should go by it. I also agree that it is anxiety, worry and such other imagined thoughts that are harmful and come in the way of responding to our intuition. Hereafter fear will be spoken of only in its negative connotations and not as God's gift for survival.

Tamo guṇa (inertia) is opposed to rajo guṇa (activity) and sattva guṇa (knowledge). For example, physical laziness does not allow us to be dynamic and mental laziness comes in the way of gaining knowledge. Fear is tāmasika, as it can immobilise both our body and thoughts. Have we not seen a person in an unenviable condition of going blank and being struck dumb when asked to talk in public?

When faced with the snake who was startled, scared and concerned, I too could have become immobile. The other reaction could have been violence from either of us. The snake could have stung me in defence or I could have hit out at it with whatever object I had at hand. Or I could have ran out. Luckily none of this happened. This was due to the grace of God, the grace of Guru and his teaching of Vedānta and the influence of solitude. Sattva guṇa came to my rescue.

*****

God resides in us as our noble thoughts (sāttvika buddhi). So thereafter He took over.

तदा शान्तस्वरूपः सुन्दररूपोऽत्यन्त-कारुणिकः शिवो मन्दस्मितः सन् उवाच - सौम्ये अर्जुन इव पण्डिता मन्यमाना बहुधा जल्पसि। पठितमूर्खलक्षणं दृश्यते त्वयि। विजाननात्मा न भवेत् अतिवादी। अहिंसा-प्रतिष्ठायां तत्सन्निधौ वैरभयत्यागः। तव वाक्यं मोहात् जातम्। अतः व्यर्थम्॥

अथ सावधानेनैकाग्रतया शृणु। अत्र भयस्य किमपि कारणं नास्ति। अविचारः कृतो बन्धो विचारेण निवर्तते। तस्मात् सम्यग् विचारं कुरु। एतद् ज्ञानमयं तपः कृत्वा ज्ञानी मोक्षं लभते। परमार्थतः व्यावहारतश्च भयनिवारणोपायः कर्तव्यः॥

tadā śānta-svarūpaḥ sundararūpo'tyanta-kāruṇikaḥ śivo mandasmitaḥ san uvāca – saumye arjuna iva paṇḍitā manyamānā bahudhā jalpasi, paṭhitamūrkhalakṣaṇaṁ dṛśyate tvayi, vijānan-ātmā na bhavet ativādī, ahiṁsā-pratiṣṭhāyāṁ tatsannidhau vaira-bhaya-tyāgaḥ, tava vākyaṁ mohāt jātam, ataḥ vyartham.

atha sāvadhānenaikāgratayā śṛṇu, atra bhayasya kimapi kāraṇaṁ nāsti, avicāraḥ kṛto bandho vicāreṇa nivartate, tasmāt samyag vicāraṁ kuru, etad jñānamayaṁ tapaḥ kṛt-vā jñānī mokṣaṁ labhate, paramārthataḥ vyāvahārataśca bhaya-nivāraṇopāyaḥ kartavyaḥ.

तदा – then; शान्तस्वरूपः – embodiment of peace; सुन्दररूपो – beautiful form; अत्यन्तकारुणिकः – very compassionate; शिवः – Śiva; मन्दस्मितः सन् – with a smile; उवाच – said; सौम्ये – dear child; अर्जुन इव – like Arjuna; पण्डिता – wise; मन्यमाना – thinking (yourself); बहुधा – a lot; जल्पसि – you talk; पठितमूर्खलक्षणं – signs of a literate fool; दृश्यते – is seen; त्वयि – in you; विजानन् आत्मा – the one who is realised; न भवेत् – does not; अतिवादी – talk much; अहिंसाप्रतिष्ठायां सन्निधौ – in the presence of a person well-established in the vow of non-injury; तत् वैरभयत्यागः – all thoughts of revenge and fear disappear; तव वाक्यं

- your words; मोहात् - from delusion; जातम् - arise; अतः - therefore; व्यर्थम्- in vain

अथ - so; सावधानेन् - with an alert; एकाग्रतया - with a focused (mind); शृणु - listen; अत्र - here; भयस्य - of fear; किमपि नास्ति - not valid; कारणम् - cause; अविचारः कृतो बन्धः - all grief and bondage arise out of either not thinking or incomplete thinking or wrong thinking; विचारेण निवर्तते - (it is) removed by right and complete thinking; तस्मात् - therefore; सम्यग् - well; विचारं कुरु - think; एतद् ज्ञानमयं तपः - this austerity of 'thinking rightly;' कृत्वा - by performing; ज्ञानी - a wise man; मोक्षं लभते - gets liberated; परमार्थतः - from the Absolute/ Supreme; व्यावहारतः - relative/practical standpoint; च - and; भयनिवारणोपायः - ways to remove fear; कर्तव्यः - must be done

Then Śiva the embodiment of peace, beauty and compassion, with a smile, said, 'Dear child, thinking yourself wise and learned like Arjuna, you talk a lot. I see the signs of a literate fool in you. The one who is Realised does not talk much. In the presence of a person well-established in the vow of non-injury, all arguments, revenge and fear disappear. Your words arise out of delusion and are therefore in vain.

So listen to me with an alert and focused mind. There is no valid cause for fear. All grief and bondage arise out of either not thinking or incomplete thinking or wrong thinking. It is removed by right and complete thinking. Therefore think well. By performing this austerity of 'right thinking' a wise man gets liberated. From the Absolute/Supreme and the relative practical standpoint one should think of the ways to remove fear.

Silence speaks: As long as we talk, we do not hear the voice of God. When our mind stops chattering, silence speaks. A devotee would visit the temple daily, say his regular prayers and return. He considered God his friend, so he would pour out his problems along with the prayers. One day he thought, 'I have been talking each day to God. For a change, let me hear what He has to speak.' So that day he did not chant his prayers or talk of his life. But he found that his mind was chattering and he could not hear God's words. He finally silenced his mind and realised God as non-dual peace and auspiciousness (śāntaṁ śivaṁ advaitam).

The inner voice is also referred to as the voice of wisdom, our conscience or as the higher Self. When we talk to others, we are polite, diplomatic and avoid saying words which come to our mind, if we feel they would hurt the other person. However, the inner voice tells us things exactly as they are without addition or deletion.

Śrī Kṛṣṇa's smile: Arjuna in his confusion gave a long discourse on the evils of war and dharma. Śrī Kṛṣṇa let him talk. Finally when he realised that he was deluded, he surrendered to Śrī Kṛṣṇa and asked Him for guidance and knowledge. Śrī Kṛṣṇa smiled and told Arjuna that even though he was speaking like a wise man, he was unwise as the wise do not grieve.[1] He smiled as His power of delusion (māyā śakti) did not even spare His dear friend and devotee Arjuna. Śrī Kṛṣṇa taught the *Gītā* and proved to Arjuna in many ways and from many standpoints, that there was no cause whatsoever for grief and delusion. After the teaching Arjuna says, 'By Your grace, my delusion has gone.'[2]

Śiva's smile: Like a compassionate parent Lord Śiva smiled at my unfounded fears and immature prattlings.

[1] *prajñāvādāṁśca bhāṣase ... nānuśocanti paṇḍitāḥ.* – *Gītā* 2.11
[2] *naṣṭo mohaḥ smṛtir-labdhā tvatprasādāt-mayācyuta.* – *Gītā* 18.73

In *Dāsabodha* of Samartha Rāmadāsa an entire chapter describes the characteristics of an educated fool (paḍhata mūrkha lakṣaṇa). Such a person, studies the scriptures, and advises others to follow it. He applies all that is said to others. He speaks wise words, but his foolishness persists. My words too appeared wise but were born from fear and delusion, for one who realises the Self/Truth, does not speak much – so say the scriptures.[1]

Eloquent silence: Once Mā Ānandamayī visited the Sandeepany Āśrama. Śrī Gurudev sat respectfully, as did all the other brahmacārins undergoing the Vedānta Course. There was a divine silence. Suddenly a brahmacārī asked Mā to bless all with her words. She said, 'What is there to speak?' and kept quiet. Śrī Gurudev spoke for an hour about the Truth which is beyond words and Mā said, 'That is what I meant.' Her silence was eloquent and Śrī Gurudev's eloquence indicated 'supreme silence'.

The vow of non-injury: Any vow which is followed scrupulously without exception for twelve years, becomes accomplished (siddha). Therefore, none

[1] *vijānan-ātmā na bhavet ativādī*

can have hatred, revenge, ill feelings or fear in the presence of one well-established in non-injury. Either the person leaves or his hatred leaves him.[1]

Great saints have lived in forests in the midst of wild animals without being harmed. Wild animals would dance in God-intoxication as Caitanya Mahāprabhu would sing the name of the Lord as he passed through the forest. Aṅgulimāla who had come to kill Śrī Buddha became his disciple. People with enmity towards each other would become friends in the presence of Swami Chinmayananda. If I were well-established in the vow of non-injury, neither the snake nor me, would have got scared.

Right thinking: It is said that most problems would not arise, but for a moment's thought, but a moment is a long time and thinking is a difficult process! Even though we are thinking from morning to night and from birth to death, we have not learnt 'how to think' which is even more important than 'what to think'.

[1] *ahiṁsā-pratiṣṭhāyāṁ tat vaira-tyāgaḥ* – *Yoga Sūtra* 2.35

Many just do not think, especially about the most important aspects of life, like 'who am I' or 'what is the purpose of human life'. Many think a little, think superficially or think incompletely. Thinking exhausts them quickly. Some on the other hand think in a completely lopsided way, drawing wrong conclusion and holding onto dangerous ideas like, 'It is better to be cruel, than to be a victim of cruelty'.

We should therefore think, think right and complete. That is considered as the best means to Realisation.[1]

Non-injury, humility, fearlessness (ahiṁsā, amāna, abhaya): Pride (ego), violence and fear are interrelated. What is absence of pride (amāna), absence of violence (ahiṁsā) and absence of fear (abhaya)? Pride, violence and fear are thoughts (bhāva-rūpa or vṛttis), whereas their absence is not a thought or an emotion. Lack of pride expresses as simplicity and service, absence of violence as love and kindness and lack of fear as valour and faith. But non-injury, no-pride and fearlessness are simply lack of violence, pride and fear.

---

[1] *vicāraḥ sādhanaṁ śreṣṭham – Manaḥ Śodhanam* 8

Pride, violence and fear agitate the mind, and therefore their absence calms the mind. They are human values which make us humane. They are Godly qualities which make us divine and from the highest standpoint they are the very infinite nature of Self/Truth.

The Lord therefore teaches us how to remove fear (bhaya nivāraṇa upāya), not how to cultivate fearlessness. He explains that there is no real cause of fear from different standpoints and how it should be dealt with.

2.1 Absolute Fearlessness – The Path of Knowledge

The Lord starts His teaching from the highest standpoint through the Path of Enquiry – Jñāna Yoga.

अथ परमार्थम्। ज्ञानयोगं वक्ष्यामि। द्वैतात् भयं जायते। सर्वं खल्विदं ब्रह्म। आत्मैव इदं सर्वम्। ब्रह्मैवाऽऽत्मा। नेह नानास्ति किञ्चन। अद्वयोऽहम् अनन्तोऽहं सच्चिदानन्दोऽहम् इति ज्ञात्वा अभये प्रतितिष्ठसि। अविद्यया जगज्जातं नास्ति सत्यम् इहाण्वपि। असज्जगतः भयम् अपि असदेव॥

atha paramārthaṁ, jñāna yogaṁ vakṣyāmi, dvaitāt bhayaṁ jāyate, sarvaṁ khalvidaṁ brahma, ātmaiva idaṁ sarvam, brahmaivā''tmā, neha nānāsti kiñcana, advayo'ham ananto'haṁ saccidānando'ham iti jñātvā abhaye pratitiṣṭhasi, avidyayā jagaj-jātaṁ nāsti satyam ihāṇvapi, asaj-jagataḥ bhayam api asadeva.

अथ - now (we shall review fear); **परमार्थम्** - the supreme standpoint; **ज्ञानयोगम्** - the path of Knowledge; **वक्ष्यामि** - I shall tell you; द्वैतात् - from (the sense of) duality; भयम् - fear; जायते - is born; सर्वं खल्विदं - indeed everything is; ब्रह्म - Reality (alone); आत्मैव इदं - Self alone is this; सर्वं - all; ब्रह्म-एव - the Reality (only) is; आत्मा - Self; न-इह - here not; नाना किञ्चन अस्ति - least bit of difference / duality; अद्वयः - non-dual; अहम् - I am; अनन्तः - infinite; सच्चिदानन्दः - Existence -Consciousness-Bliss; इति - thus; ज्ञात्वा - knowing; अभये - in fearlessness; प्रतितिष्ठसि - remain established; अविद्यया जातम् - born of ignorance; जगत् - world; नास्ति - not there; सत्यम् - truth; इह - here; अणु - iota; अपि - even; असज्जगतः - from an illusory world; भयमपि - even fear; असदेव - is itself illusory

Now we shall review fear from the supreme standpoint. I shall tell you Jñāna Yoga – the Path of Knowledge. Fear is born from the sense of duality. Indeed everything is the Reality alone. All is the Self alone. The Reality is the Self. There is not the least bit of difference or duality. 'I am the non-dual, infinite, Existence -Consciousness -Bliss.' Knowing thus, remain established in fearlessness. The entire world is born of ignorance and there is not an iota of truth to it. The fear born from an illusory world is itself illusory.

Bhaya Yoga: 'Bhoga' unites us with the world and 'yoga' with God. Arjuna's grief made him surrender to God and He taught Arjuna the celestial song – the *Bhagavad-gītā*. The first chapter of *Gītā* is therefore called Arjuna-viṣāda-yoga – the Yoga of Arjuna's Grief. My fear connected me with Lord Śiva's teaching (bhaya-yoga) and therefore became a blessing. With His blessings may I connect with God in all ways, always (sarvabhāvena sarvadā), whatever be my emotions or thoughts or circumstances of love, anger, doubts or conflict.

The Lord speaks of how to remove fear by following the Path of Knowledge, Meditation and Devotion. The teaching begins with the Path of Knowledge.

Duality causes fear: The very existence of another, however big or small, creates the possibility of fear. If anything is considered even a little different from me, like my own shadow, it may cause fear.

How far is God from me or how close is God to me? Even if one says that He is the closest, one admits to a distance, however small. Only when one says, 'He is me', that all possibility of fear, even of God goes. Many people worship in fear and have the concept of an angry God, a jealous God or a revengeful God. This is because they feel distant from Him.

The scriptures say that the infinite Truth alone exists, One without a second (ekam eva advitīyaṁ brahma). There cannot be two infinities or even infinity + 1 (as all is included in infinity). Also if the infinite Truth is different from me, it can become the cause of infinite fears in me. The scriptures assure us that the infinite Truth alone is the pure Self and that there is not the slightest distance or difference in them.[1] If I create the slightest of difference between God and me, I can become scared of God. For example, some are frightened of their own shadow, and start imagining it to be a sinister person following them step by step. Some are scared of their own thoughts which persecute them day and night. I too can become scared of God if I think Him as a sinister presence, a judgemental Lord or a persecuting entity.

It is difficult to accept that nothing exists except the infinite Truth/Self. Does that mean that the world does not exist at all? But I do experience the world. I see it as different from myself. It is of infinite variety

[1] *tat-tvam-eva, tvam-eva tat – Kaivalya Upaniṣad* 1.16

and expanse. No wonder I am plagued by hundreds of fears due to it.

The Lord says that if you see the world, then its experience is only relatively real, not absolutely so. It is an appearance created due to ignorance of our infinite nature. An ignorance created illusory world, cannot cause real fear. Our fear too is born of ignorance and equally illusory. For example, the dream lion, the fear it causes and every other object and being in the dream world, are equally dream -like and unreal.

*****

What is ignorance and how can that be the cause of the world?

काऽविद्या? सत्यावरणम् असत्यारोपणं च अविद्या। आवरण-मात्रेण बन्धनं नास्ति। अध्यासात् दुःखानुभवः। अध्यासः आवरणानन्तरं भवति। अनावरणात् अध्यासः नश्यति। सत्यदर्शने यतिः विमुक्तो भवति निर्भयो भवति॥

kā'vidyā? satyāvaraṇam asatyāropaṇaṁ ca avidyā, āvaraṇa-mātreṇa bandhanaṁ nāsti, adhyāsāt duḥkhānubhavaḥ, adhyāsaḥ āvaraṇānantaraṁ bhavati, anāvaraṇāt adhyāsaḥ naśyati, satyadarśane yatiḥ vimukto bhavati nirbhayo bhavati.

का – what (is); अविद्या - ignorance; सत्यावरणम् – veiling of Truth; असत्यारोपणं – superimposition of the false; च – and; अविद्या - ignorance; आवरणमात्रेण – by mere veiling; बन्धनम् – bondage; नास्ति – does not cause; अध्यासात् – from superimposition (of the false); दुःखानुभवः – gives the experience of sorrow; अध्यासः – superimposition; आवरणानन्तरम् – after the Truth is veiled; भवति – takes place; अनावरणात् – due to removal of veiling; अध्यासः नश्यति – superimposition is destroyed; सत्यदर्शने – on realising the Truth; यतिः – the seeker; विमुक्तो भवति – gets liberated; निर्भयो भवति – becomes fearless

What is ignorance? The veiling of Truth and the superimposition of the false is called ignorance. The veiling alone does not cause bondage. It is the superimposition of the false that gives the experience of sorrow. Superimposition takes place only after the Truth is veiled. When the veiling is removed, the superimposition is destroyed. On realising the Truth the seeker gets liberated and becomes fearless.

Science proposes the Big Bang and such other theories, the primordial matter or one unifying energy as the cause of the world. Religion postulates God to be the cause of the world. Vedānta states that ignorance is the cause of the world – ignorance of our infinite nature. This does not contradict anyone's views from whatever standpoint they talk.

Ignorance is also called māyā, the Lord's power of delusion. It is not an entity, a material, an object with a form. It is simply the lack of knowledge. It has two powers – the veiling power (āvaraṇa śakti) and the projecting power (vikṣepa śakti). The veiling power first veils the Truth. Due to it, we do not see what actually 'is'. Thereafter, the projecting power (vikṣepa śakti) projects what is not there. By itself non-apprehension of the Truth does not cause us any problem. No one has any problem in the deep sleep state where there is total ignorance of ourselves and no projection of the world. Also non-apprehension – 'I don't know', is the same in all of us. Each of us projects their own mis-apprehensions and they cause sorrow, fear and bondage.

Ironically, we will use the example of the snake vision superimposed on the rope to explain this point further. Not seeing the rope is common to three persons who enter the garden. One assumes it is a snake and runs away in fear. Another also thinks it is a snake, but bravely tries to face it, since he is sure it cannot be poisonous. The third laughs at both and says that it is only a crack in the ground. The second person gets convinced by the third and sees it as a crack in the ground. In the meantime the first person returns with a stick and starts beating the snake he thinks he sees. That is when all realise that it is a rope.

Misapprehensions are many; one may cause fear, another sorrow, one can replace another, but all are equally false. Only in the knowledge of the substratum will the superimposed thoughts disappear, not by substituting one superimposition with another. Also, if we remove the superimposition, but still do not see the substratum, the chance of superimposing something else is always there. Therefore only with the removal of the ignorance by right knowledge, will we be truly free from bondage, sorrow and fear. Such fearlessness is not like the valour of a person brave enough to face the snake, but the fearlessness of one who has seen the snake vision as false.

Vivekacūḍāmaṇi says that we should remove our superimpositions and see the underlying Truth (svādhyāsāpanayaṁ kuru). As long as the superimpositions occupy our mind, we will not think of finding their root. Therefore it is important to understand the nature of superimpositions.

*****

What is superimposition and how can we remove it? The Lord says –

कोऽध्यासः? अत्यन्ताभावेऽपि भावारोपो अध्यासः रज्जुसर्पादिवत्। सत्ताध्यासात् भयम्। सदसदविवेकात् किञ्चित् वस्तुरस्ति स्वतन्त्रं तिष्ठति मद्भिन्नमस्ति आत्मवत् सत्यमस्ति इति सत्ताध्यासः॥

अबाधितम् एकं वस्तु सत्। तद्विपरीतम् असत्। आत्मनो अभावोऽसिद्धः। जगतोऽभावः सुषुप्तौ प्रसिद्धः। तस्मात् सद्रूपोऽहं मदन्यत् किमपि नास्ति अस्ति चेत् मिथ्यैव इति ज्ञात्वा निर्भया भव॥

ko'dhyāsaḥ? atyantābhāve'pi bhāvāropo adhyāsaḥ rajjusarpādivat, sattādhyāsāt bhayam, sadasadavivekāt kiñcit vasturasti svatantraṁ tiṣṭhati madbhinnamasti ātmavat satyamasti iti sattādhyāsaḥ.

abādhitam ekaṁ vastu sat, tadviparītam asat, ātmano abhāvo'siddhaḥ, jagato'bhāvaḥ suṣuptau prasiddhaḥ, tasmāt sadrūpo'haṁ madanyat kimapi nāsti asti cet mithyaiva iti jñātvā nirbhayā bhava.

कः - what is; अध्यासः - superimposition; अत्यन्ताभावे - in its total absence; अपि - even; भावारोपः - giving existence to a thing; अध्यासः - superimposition; रज्जु-सर्पादिवत् - like seeing a snake in a rope and so on; सत्ताध्यासात् - from 'the superimposition of existence'; भयम् - (causes) fear; सदसद्-अविवेकात् - due to lack of discrimination between the real and unreal; किञ्चित् - some; वस्तुरस्ति - exists a thing; स्वतन्त्रं तिष्ठति - has its own independent existence; मद्भिन्नाम्अस्ति - it exists apart from me; आत्मवत् - like mine; सत्यम्अस्ति - it is real; इति - thus (is called); सत्ताध्यासः - superimposition of existence

अबाधितम् - that which remains un-negated; एकं वस्तु - one thing; सत् - Truth / Existence; तद्विपरीतम् - other than that (everything else is); असत् - false / non-existent; आत्मनः - (of the) Self; अभावः - non -existence; असिद्धः - can never be; जगतः - (of the) world; अभावः - absence; सुषुप्तौ - in the deep sleep; प्रसिद्धः - is experienced (by all); तस्मात् - therefore; सद्रूपोऽहम् - I am of the nature of pure Existence/Truth; मदन्यत् - apart from me; किमपि नास्ति - nothing exists; अस्ति चेत् - if it (appears) to exist; मिथ्यैव - it is an illusion; इति ज्ञात्वा - knowing thus; निर्भया भव - be fearless

What is superimposition? Giving existence to a thing, even in its total absence, like seeing a snake in a rope, is called superimposition. The 'superimposition of Existence' causes fear. Due to lack of discrimination between the Real (Existence) and unreal (non-existence), the thought that – something exists, it has its own independent existence, it exists apart from me, and its existence is real like mine – is called 'superimposition of Existence'.

Truth or Existence is that which remains un-negated. Other than that, everything else is false or non-existent. The Self can never be non-existent whereas, the non-existence or absence of the world is experienced by all in the deep sleep state. Therefore I am of the nature of pure Existence/Truth. Other than me nothing exists. If it appears to exist then it is an illusion. Knowing thus be fearless.

What is superimposition? The idea of existence of a thing, where it is totally absent is called superimposition. *Vivekacūḍāmaṇi* calls it the thought or vision that it is, where it is not (atasmin tad -buddhi). We are quite expert at this as we have practised and perfected it over lifetimes and do so quite unconsciously, also in our daily transactions. We often say, 'I don't know him, but I think he must be ..., he should be ..., he could be ...'. We make educated guesses or informed predictions which are not based on any education or information.

Basic superimpositions: The two main false notions that we have are the notion of Self on the not -Self and the notion of Reality on the unreal world (anātmani ātmabuddhi and jagati satyatva-buddhi). I consider myself to be the body-mind-intellect, and the world to be absolutely real. These notions lead to endless other projections. 'I am fair, tall, fat ...', 'I am an Indian, Brāhmaṇa middle-class ...', 'I am intelligent, talented, engineer ...', 'All are selfish, money makes the world go around, ...'. It is these projections that cause bondages, sorrow and fear.

All superimpositions spring from the lack of right thinking (aviveka). No superimposition is possible without a substratum on which it is projected, like the snake vision on the rope. Discrimination between the superimposed and its substratum (ādhāra-ādheya-viveka) will remove the superimposition – the unreal and bring to light the substratum – the real. The infinite Truth/Self is the substratum of all the superimpositions. It is of the nature of Existence-Consciousness-Bliss. For the sake of reflection, we can say that there are three basic superimpositions– the superimposition of Existence (sattā-adhyāsa), the superimposition of Consciousness (cid-adhyāsa) and the superimposition of happiness (sukha-adhyāsa). Each will now be discussed.

Superimposition of Existence (sattādhyāsa): On any object – starting from the body and the mind, to things and beings of the world, heaven, hell or other realms or cosmoses, any other concept or theory – we impose the following notions: the object exists, it has independent existence and is different from me and it is as real as me. For example, the snake exists, (it 'is'); even if I die through snake bite, it will exist (independent existence), it is outside in the altar and I am seeing it (different from me) and it is very much real, and its sting could cause real pain (as real as me).

However, can there be many Existences? Existing objects can be many, but the 'is-ness' in them is the same. Is-ness underlies both the presence and absence of objects. For example, there 'is' a cat and there 'is' no one in the room. Also Truth/ Existence is infinite and there cannot be two infinities.

Also Truth/Existence (sat) is that which cannot be contradicted, which ever 'is', unchanging in the past, present and future. Also, I can never experience my absence and the 'I am' (existence) in each experience remains ever the same. That means I am the infinite Existence which is, was and ever will be.

Other than Truth/Existence (sat) everything is either asat or mithyā. 'Asat' is that which never ever existed, in the past, present or future like a barren woman's child. Mithyā is that which appears to exist, but gets contradicted like the blueness in the sky. The body, mind and the world are asat or mithyā as they appear (are experienced), but get contradicted (and are not experienced) in the deep sleep state. Then why should I, who is of the nature of Existence, be afraid of a non-existent or an illusory snake. It's very existence depends on me. How can I be scared of a snake whom 'I' have projected and given existence to?

Once, Sage Vasiṣṭha was teaching Śrī Rāma in the forest. He said, 'The infinite Truth alone is real and the world is an illusion.' (brahma satyam jagat mithyā). At that time, a wild elephant came. Sage Vasiṣṭha ran and Śrī Rāma followed him. Later Śrī Rāma asked, "O

Guro, if the whole world is an illusion, why did you run from the illusory elephant?" He replied, "Even my running was an illusion!" We may accept that the outside world is an illusion, but it is difficult for us to think that our body and its activities and our mind and its joys, sorrows, tensions and fears are equally illusory. The sorrows of others seem more distant and less real than the pains of my body and the hurts in my mind. But they are not so. They all get contradicted. I the pure Self alone remains uncontradicted, and therefore is real.

*****

What is superimposition of Consciousness?

चिदध्यासात् भयम्। चिज्जडयोः अविवेकात् मदन्यस्मात् चेतनस्य कल्पना चिदध्यासः। चित् स्वयं विभाति अथान्यानि भासयेत् साधनं विना। आत्मा स्वप्रकाशः तस्मात् चैतन्यमेव। अनात्मा परप्रकाश्यः तस्मात् जडम्। जडे आत्मचेतनस्य अभिव्यक्तिः जीवनं उच्यते। जीवति इति जीवः॥

तथा जीवदृष्ट्या भयं कुतः? यथा प्रतिबिम्बस्य प्रतिबिम्बात्। आत्मदृष्ट्याऽपि भयं कुतः? यथा बिम्बस्य प्रतिबिम्बवत् सूर्यवत्। चिद्रूपोऽहं नास्ति भिन्नं चितः किञ्चित् मामैवभान्तमनुभाति सर्वं नाहं जीवो परात्मेति ज्ञातश्चेत् निर्भयो भवेत् इति प्रसिद्धम्॥

cidadhyāsāt bhayam, cijjaḍayoḥ avivekāt madanyasmāt cetanasya kalpanā cidadhyāsaḥ, cit svayaṁ vibhāti athānyāni bhāsayet sādhanaṁ vinā, ātmā svaprakāśaḥ tasmāt caitanyameva, anātmā paraprakāśyaḥ tasmāt jaḍam, jaḍe ātmacetanasya abhivyaktiḥ jīvanaṁ ucyate, jīvati iti jīvaḥ.

tathā jīvadṛṣṭyā bhayaṁ kutaḥ? yathā pratibimbasya pratibimbāt, ātmadṛṣṭyā'pi bhayaṁ kutaḥ? yathā bimbasya pratibimbavat sūryavat, cidrūpo'haṁ nāsti bhinnaṁ citaḥ kiñcit māmaivabhāntam-anubhāti sarvaṁ nāhaṁ jīvo parātmeti jñātaścet nirbhayo bhavet iti prasiddham.

चिद्ध्यासात् - due to the 'superimposition of Consciousness;' भयम् - fear (is caused); चिज्जडयोः - between the Consciousness and inert; अविवेकात् - due to the lack of discrimination; मदन्यस्मात् - apart from me; चेतनस्य - of Consciousness; कल्पना - the thought; चिदध्यासः - (is called) superimposition; चित् - Consciousness; स्वयं विभाति - is self-illumined; अथान्यानि भासयेत् - (and) illumines everything else; साधनं विना - without any aid; आत्मा - the Self (is); स्वप्रकाशः - self-shining; तस्मात् - therefore; चैतन्यमेव - (of the) nature of Consciousness; अनात्मा - the not-Self; परप्रकाश्यः - needs something else to illumine; तस्मात् - (and is) therefore; जडम् - inert;

जडे - (through) an inert medium.; आत्मचेतनस्य - of Consciousness; अभिव्यक्तिः - the manifestation; जीवनम् उच्यते - is called life; जीवति - one who has life; इति - is called; जीवः - the individual living being

तथा - therefore; जीवदृष्ट्या - from the standpoint of the individual; भयं कुतः - how can there be fear?; यथा - just as; प्रतिबिम्बस्य - of a reflection; प्रतिबिम्बात् - from another reflection (how can fear arise?); आत्मदृष्ट्या अपि - even from the standpoint of the Self; भयं कुतः - how can there be fear?; यथा - just as; बिम्बस्य - of the reflection; प्रतिबिम्बवत् - like its own reflection (how can fear arise?); सूर्यवत् - the sun; चिद्रूपोऽहं - (therefore)' I am of the nature of pure Consciousness' नास्ति भिन्नं - there is no other / apart from; चितः किञ्चित् - the Consciousness; मामैव-भान्तम्मअनुभाति सर्वम् - illumined by me all else shines; नाहं जीवः - I am not the individual being; परात्मेति - (but) the supreme Consciousness; ज्ञातश्चेत् - knowing thus; निर्भयो भवेत् - (one) becomes fearless; इति - thus; प्रसिद्धम् - is known

Fear is caused due to the 'superimposition of Consciousness'. Due to the lack of discrimination between the Consciousness and inert, the thought that a conscious entity exists apart

from me is called 'superimposition of Consciousness'. Consciousness is self-evident and illumines everything else without any aid. The Self is self-shining and is therefore of the nature of Consciousness. The not-Self needs something else to illumine it and is therefore inert. The manifestation of Consciousness through an inert medium is called life. The one who has life is called the individual living being.

Therefore from the standpoint of the individual, how can there be fear? How can one reflection fear another reflection? Even from the standpoint of the Self, how can there be fear? Just as the sun does not fear its own reflection, how can the Self that gets reflected as the individual, fear its own reflection? Therefore I am of the nature of pure Consciousness and there is no other Consciousness apart from me. Illumined by me all else shines. 'I am not the individual being but the Supreme Consciousness.' Knowing thus one becomes fearless.

Superimposition of Consciousness (cid-adhyāsa): The notion that a Consciousness exists independent of me, different from me and is as real as me is superimposition of Consciousness. For example, I think that the snake is aware, its awareness is different from mine and its awareness is as real as mine.

This occurs due to lack of discrimination between Consciousness and the inert (cid-jaḍa-aviveka).

Consciousness is that which illumines or knows itself and illumines others without aid. For example, the sun is self-luminous and in its light even the clouds that hide it are seen. The Self, 'I' is self-illumined. I do not need others, my own eyes or mind to know that 'I am'. Also, 'I know' the thoughts of my mind, the condition of my body and the world of objects. Therefore the Self is Consciousness.

The inert is that which does not know itself and illumines others with borrowed awareness. For example, the book does not know that it is a book. The eyes illumine the book, but do not see or know themselves. The mind knows the condition of the eyes and can conceive of everything under the sun, but cannot know itself. 'I' know the thoughts and the thoughts know objects in 'my' light or awareness. Therefore the objects of the world, the body and the mind are all inert.

But, what about sentient beings? Does not each of them have a Consciousness and life? Yes they do, but is the Consciousness different in all? Life is the manifestation of Consciousness in the gross body, through the medium of the subtle body (mind), just like light is the manifestation of electricity in the bulb, through the medium of the filament. Just as the electricity is one in all the electric gadjets, Consciousness is the same in all living beings.

The sun reflects on solar panels which can in turn illumine a bulb or heat water. But their ability to illumine and heat is borrowed from the sun. The sun is one and reflects in millions of reflecting surfaces, simultaneously, appearing different according to the surface or medium in which it reflects. Can the reflections claim to have their own independent existence and light apart from the sun? Are they different from the sun's light? Do they have a reality apart from the sun?

Now from the standpoint of Consciousness/ Self, how can I be afraid of the inert world of objects which have no awareness and existence of their own? How can I be scared of one of my own reflections in the snake body? Even if I consider myself to be a sentient being, how can I, as one reflection, be scared of another reflection of Consciousness in the snake body, both being dependent for their very existence on Consciousness?

A king on his way to the court, passed by the hall of mirrors. He admired himself reflected in some mirrors and laughed at his distorted reflections in some concave and convex mirrors. The king's dog entered the same hall and was terrified when faced with hundreds of dog reflections coming towards him in different shapes and sizes.

Alexander was passing through Punjab on his return after his conquest of India. As others stood in respect, a Bābājī (saint) was sleeping in his chārapāī (cot) unconcerned. Alexander ordered that he be taken as a prisoner. Alexander noticed that there was not even a bit of fear, anger or hatred emotions, he was used to seeing on the face of people about to be killed. He asked, "Are you not scared of dying? I am about to kill you." Bābājī said, "You cannot kill me. You can only kill this already perishing body. I am the Self in you. I am the eternal Existence and Consciousness in all."

*****

What is superimposition of Happiness and how will it go?

सुखाध्यासात् भयम्। सुखदुःखयोः अविवेकात् वस्तुनि सुखारोपः सुखाध्यासः। ततः परतन्त्रता भयं च दुःखं च। न अल्पे सुखमस्ति। यो वै भूमा तत्सुखम्। देशकाल-वस्त्वपरिच्छिन्नं भूमा। आत्मैव भूमा। आनन्दोऽहम् अनन्तोऽहम् अद्वयोऽहं स्वतन्त्रोऽहम् इति मत्वा अभया भव॥

sukhādhyāsāt bhayam, sukhaduḥkhayoḥ avivekāt vastuni sukhāropaḥ sukhādhyāsaḥ, tataḥ paratantratā bhayaṁ ca duḥkhaṁ ca, na alpe sukhamasti, yo vai bhūmā tatsukham, deśakāla-vastvaparicchinnaṁ bhūmā, ātmaiva bhūmā, ānando'ham ananto'ham advayo'haṁ svatantro'ham iti matvā abhayā bhava.

सुखाध्यासात् - from the superimposition of happiness; भयम् - fear arises; सुखदुःखयोः अविवेकात् - due to lack of discrimination between happiness and sorrow; वस्तुनि - on objects; सुखारोपः - to impose joy; सुखाध्यासः - is called 'superimposition of happiness;' ततः - thereafter; परतन्त्रता - one becomes dependent (on the object); भयं च दुःखं च - fears its loss and becomes unhappy; नास्ति - there is no; अल्पे - in finitude or finite objects; सुखम् - joy; यो वै - that which; भूमा - (is) infinite; तत्सुखम् - that is Bliss; देश-काल-वस्तु-अपरिच्छिन्नम् - that which is unconditioned by space, time and objects; भूमा - is infinite; आत्मैव - the Self alone; भूमा - is infinite; आनन्दोऽहम् - I am of the nature of Bliss; अनन्तोऽहम् - I am infinite; अद्वयोऽहम् - I am non-dual; स्वतन्त्रोऽहम् - I am independent; इति मत्वा - having known thus; अभया - fearless; भव - be

Fear arises from the 'superimposition of Happiness'. Due to lack of discrimination between happiness and sorrow, to superimpose joy on objects is called 'superimposition of happiness'. Thereafter one becomes dependent on the object, fears its loss and becomes unhappy. There is no joy in finitude or finite objects. That which is infinite is supreme Bliss. That which is unconditioned by space, time and objects is Infinite. The Self alone is Infinite. Therefore I am of the nature of infinite, non -dual, independent, unconditioned Bliss. Knowing thus be fearless.

Superimposition of Bliss (sukha-adhyāsa): The notion that there is happiness in objects, its source is independent and different from me and it is as real as me is called 'superimposition of happiness'. This occurs due to lack of discrimination between true happiness and sorrow (sukha-duḥkha-aviveka).

All of us without exception want happiness. This itself shows that I feel that I am incomplete (apurṇo'haṁ) and that something else will make me fulfilled and happy. The minute I superimpose happiness on any object or being, I desire it or want it. The more the joy superimposed, the more intense the desire. The more the objects on which it is superimposed the more the number of desires. If I get the object, I want more of it, I become attached, possessive, demanding ... If I do not get it, I become depressed, jealous, dejected ... Even when I superimpose sorrow on an object or being, I run away from it, hate it, want to destroy it ... Either way my joy and sorrow are dependent on the object, being or circumstance.

Dependency itself causes sorrow and fear (sarvaṁ paravaśaṁ duḥkhaṁ). We therefore pray to God, 'Let me die before I become physically dependent in old age.' We also do not want to depend on our children financially in our old age.

True Happiness: Let us think what is true happiness and what is the source of true happiness. That which is infinite (has no limit of time, space or objects), alone can be the source of true happiness. That which is itself finite, gets contradicted or comes and goes, can never be the source of true happiness. Therefore that which is Existence-Consciousness, the infinite Self, which never gets negated, alone can be the true source of happiness.

We all want eternal and infinite happiness, and that is why we want every joy to last for ever. 'The king and the queen lived happily ever after' alone is considered a happy ending. That which is eternal and infinite alone can be a source of infinite happiness. Therefore the infinite Truth/Self alone is Bliss.

Also true happiness puts an end to all sorrows (duḥkhāntaṁ ca nigacchati). What we experience through objects, beings and circumstances, makes us forget our pains for a time or gets rid of some sorrows, but it does not put an end to all our sorrows, for all times. In the gain of the infinite alone can all sorrows end, as there remains nothing more to be gained. When I know that I am the source of all happiness and I am full and complete, will I then beg for joy from finite things or beings who only reflect my inner Bliss? Knowing thus, I become totally independent of them and therefore fearless.

A dog hid a juicy bone from his rivals. It sucked it dry, when it was alone. Thereafter it kept sucking till his mouth started bleeding. He thought that the juice (blood) was from the bone and the bone was the reason for the cause of the joy and also the pain in his mouth.

Once a saint Ānandaghana (the name means one who is a mass of Bliss) was approached by the elder queen of the kingdom, with a problem, 'The king favours the younger queen.' He asked her to wear a locket with a written note. Some days later the younger queen came with a problem, 'Now the king favours the elder queen.' The saint asked both of them to read the note in the locket together. It was written, 'What does it matter to Ānandaghana if the king meets or does not meet the queen?'[1] His joy is not dependent on any object, being or circumstance. He knows that he is the sole source of all joy in the world. Everyone is enjoying but a wee bit of the infinite Bliss which is his own true nature. The Realised Master therefore rejoices in the joy of all, remaining always full and complete. He does not fear anyone, as none can take away or add to his joy. The infinite ocean of Bliss does not increase or decrease with all the rivers pouring their waters of joy or sorrow into it or the tons of waters evaporating, it being the sole source of all waters.

[1] *rājā rāṇī ko mile, to ānandaghana ko kyā,*
rājā rāṇī ko nahi mile, phir bhi ānandaghana ko kyā.

2.2 Absolute Fearlessness – The Path of Meditation

Lord Śiva, who ever remains in meditation, now teaches the Path of Meditation to overcome fear.

अथ ध्यानयोगः। भयं मनोधर्मः। स्वरूपे भयस्य लेशमपि नास्ति। समाधेः अभ्यासात् मनसो ह्यमनीभावे द्वैतं नैव-उपलभ्यते। दृश्यानुविद्धः शब्दानुविद्धश्च समाधी। अथवा मनसः उद्भव-सन्धि-लयस्थाने समाधानम्॥

ततोऽभयं प्रतिष्ठां विन्दति। ध्यायतो विषयान्पुंसः सङ्गस्तेषूपजायते। पदार्थवासना-दार्ढ्यं बन्ध इत्यभिधीयते। सङ्कल्पजाले गलिते स्वरूपमवशिष्यते। अवेदनं विदुर्योगं येन योगी निर्भयो भवेत्॥

atha dhyānayogaḥ, bhayaṁ manodharmaḥ, svarūpe bhayasya leśamapi nāsti, samādheḥ abhyāsāt manaso hyamanībhāve dvaitaṁ naiva-upalabhyate, dṛśyānuviddhaḥ śabdānuviddhaśca samādhī, athavā manasaḥ udbhava-sandhi-laya-sthāne samādhānam.

tato'bhayaṁ pratiṣṭhāṁ vindati, dhyāyato viṣayānpuṁsaḥ saṅgas-teṣūpajāyate, padārtha-vāsanā-dārḍhyaṁ bandha ityabhidhīyate, saṅkalpajāle galite svarūpam-avaśiṣyate, avedanaṁ vidur-yogaṁ yena yogī nirbhayo bhavet.

अथ - now (I shall); ध्यानयोगः - (describe) the path of meditation; भयम् - fear (exists); मनोधर्मः - (as a thought) in the mind; स्वरूपे - in (our) true nature; भयस्य - of fear; लेशमपि - even a trace; नास्ति - is not there; समाधेः अभ्यासात् - by the practice of meditation; मनसः - of mind; हि - indeed; अमनीभावे - state of no-mind; द्वैतं नैवोपलभ्यते - all duality ceases; दृश्यानुविद्धः - associated with the seen; शब्दानुविद्धः - associated with words; च - and; समाधी - meditation; अथवा - alternately; मनसः - of the mind; उद्भव-सन्धि-लय-स्थाने - (where) the thoughts originate, the gap in between thoughts or where they merge; समाधानम् - absorption

ततः - thereby; अभयम् - fearless; प्रतिष्ठाम् - established (in the substratum of thoughts); विन्दति - gets; ध्यायतो - when broods over; विषयान् - the objects; पुंसः - man; सङ्गः - attachment; तेषू - into them; उपजायते - is born; पदार्थवासना दार्ढ्यम् - (this) strong impression / attachment for objects; बन्धः - bondage; इति-अभिधीयते

– is called; सङ्कल्पजाले गलिते – when the web of thoughts and desires for objects ends; स्वरूपम्-अवशिष्यते – our true nature (free of desires and objects) remains; अवेदनम् – state beyond thoughts; विदुः योगम् – Yoga is; येन – by which; योगी – the Yogī; निर्भयो भवेत् – becomes fearless

Now I shall describe Dhyāna Yoga – the Path of Meditation. Fear exists as a thought in the mind. In our true nature (which is beyond the mind) there is not even a trace of fear. By the practice of meditation the mind attains a state of no-mind and all duality ceases. Meditation is of two types – associated with the seen and associated with words. Alternately one may absorb the mind where the thoughts origin, the gap in-between thoughts or where they merge.

Thereby one gets established in the substratum of thoughts which is fearless. When man broods over objects he gets attached to them. This strong impression or strong attachment for objects is called bondage. When the web of thoughts and desires for objects ends, our true nature (free of desires and objects) remains. Yoga is a state beyond thoughts by (attaining) which the Yogī becomes fearless.

Dhyāna Yoga: Likes-dislikes, distractions-agitations, anger-greed, sorrows-fears ... all exist in the mind.

There is not even a trace of them in the infinite Self/ Truth. By the practice of meditation, the meditator goes into a state of absorption beyond all thoughts and dualities (nirvikalpa samādhi). Once he realises his infinite nature, even when he is out of that state, he does not identify with the thoughts and remains unaffected by them.

Swami Akhandananda Maharaja would serve a great saint, who occasionally displayed anger. When asked the reason, he said, 'You come, serve and go away, unasked by me; similarly anger comes, stays and goes away. It has nothing to do with me!' Realised Masters are indeed unaffected by any thoughts.

Jñāna and Dhyāna: The Path of Knowledge involves inquiry (vicāra), discrimination (viveka) and firm ascertainment (dṛḍha niścaya). The very determination of the Truth and the falsification of the false gives Liberation from the false and abidance in the Truth.

The Path of Meditation involves practice – practise with right understanding. The practice is of owning one's own true nature. The meditator has to strengthen the thought, 'I am the infinite Truth' again and again and abide in this knowledge. It is also called brahma-abhyāsa or nididhyāsana.

One fine morning, for no rhyme or reason, Amthābhāī started thinking that he was a rat. The psychiatrist through many sessions convinced him, that he was Amthābhāī. He then said, 'I now know that I am Amthābhāī, but does the huge black cat in the neighbour's house know that I am not a rat!' Alas! In his heart, he still feels, he is a rat!

Meditation is a practice through which we remove the habitual error of mistaking ourselves to be finite, and the world to be real. Since the identification with the finite has been strengthened over many lifetimes, it takes determined, regular and rigorous practice of meditation to remove it.

The scriptures teach us many techniques of practising meditation. Lord Śiva elaborates on three of them.

1. **Meditation with the seen:** A person sits on the banks of the river and watches the flow of water.

Similarly, the meditator watches the flow of thoughts as a witness (sākṣī). He does not analyse or categorise, accept or reject, qualify or quantify, like or dislike, associate or connect with any thoughts. He just observes them without reacting or responding to them. By this practice, the mind becomes calmer. As the feeling of being the witnessing Consciousness becomes stronger with practice, the thoughts reduce further and finally vanish altogether. Since there remain no thoughts to witness there is abidance in Consciousness/Self. Thereafter even when there are thoughts, they are understood to be the not-Self, and do not affect the Realised Master.

2. **Meditation with words:** The meditator takes the support of words like, 'I am the infinite Truth' (ahaṁ brahmāsmi), 'I am unattached (asaṅgo'haṁ) ...' He connects himself to the meaning of these words – not the literal meaning but the implied meaning. The words then drop and the thought 'I am infinite' remains. When this thought matures by the force of practice, it too drops and the meditator attains a state of non-dual Bliss, his own infinite nature (nirvikalpa samādhi).

Once, before Śrī Gurudev's Vedānta class, one devotee was melodiously singing, 'sarvaṁ brahmamayaṁ re re sarvaṁ brahmamayam ...' (all is Brahma, indeed all is Brahma). Śrī Gurudev remarked, 'Are re! This is not for singing and clapping, but for meditation and Realisation!'

3. **Meditation with thoughts:** Thoughts emerge and merge from the infinite Truth/Self along with the 'I thought'. The meditator focusses on 'that' from where the thoughts or the 'I thought' emerge and merge. Some focus their attention on the gap between two thoughts. Since the thoughts are too many and too fast, a mantra is used. As the mantra is chanted, the mind is to be focussed on that Truth from which the mantra emerges and into which it merges or on the gap between the two mantras, ... om ... om ... om ... or om namaḥ śivāya ... om namaḥ śivāya ... Any mantra can serve the purpose, especially the mantra of our favourite form of the Lord (iṣṭa-deva-mantra). As we practise, the gap or wordless, soundless and thoughtless state increases in duration. By the force of practice the sounds, words, and thoughts end and the meditator attains his infinite nature (nirvikalpa samādhi).

Beware! The benign destructive power of meditation: Besides its many side and extra effects, the practice of meditation quietens the mind, exhausts the vāsanās, loosens the hold of our inherent tendencies and reduces our desires, passions and volitions. Meditation or constant brooding on worldly objects and beings increases our attachments, desires ... and finally leads to the destruction of our intellect.[1] Meditation on the divine virtues and attributes of the Lord (saguṇa dhyāna) destroys our vices (durguṇa). Meditation on the attributeless Truth (nirguṇa dhyāna) destroys our ego and ignorance (ajñāna-ahaṅkāra-nāśa). Destructive minds also use the power of meditation to kill others as in pre-meditated murder. Sage Patañjali recommends meditation to destroy the five agitators of the mind[2] namely, ignorance, ego, likes, dislikes and fear of death.

1 *dhyāyato viṣayān-puṁsaḥ ... buddhināśāt-praṇaśyati* – *Gītā* 2.62/63
2 *dhyāna-heyās-tadvṛttayaḥ* – *Yoga Sūtras* 2.11

2.3 Absolute Fearlessness – The Path of Devotion

The compassionate Lord Śiva now teaches the easier Path of Devotion to overcome fear.

अथ भक्तियोगः। अहंमतिकृतः भेदो भयं च। बलिराजा इव परमेश्वराय प्रीत्या अहन्ता-ममता-समर्पणं भक्तिः। मृत्युभयं सर्वप्रसिद्धम्। स्वरसवाही विदुषोऽपि तथारूढोऽभिनिवेशः। तथा श्री रमणेन प्रोक्तम् - मृत्युञ्जयं मृत्युभियाश्रितानाम् अहं मतिर्मृत्युमुपैति पूर्वम्। तत्र को मोहः कः शोकः किं भयमेकत्वं अनुपश्यतः॥

atha bhaktiyogaḥ, ahaṁmatikṛtaḥ bhedo bhayaṁ ca, balirājā iva parameśvarāya prītyā ahantā-mamatā-samarpaṇaṁ bhaktiḥ, mṛtyubhayaṁ sarvaprasiddham, svarasavāhī viduṣo'pi tathārūḍho'bhiniveśaḥ, tathā śrī ramaṇena proktam – mṛtyuñjayaṁ mṛtyubhiyāśritānām ahaṁ matir-mṛtyum-upaiti pūrvam, tatra ko mohaḥ kaḥ śokaḥ kiṁ bhayam-ekatvam anupaśyataḥ.

अथ - now (I shall); भक्तियोगः - the Path of Devotion; अहंमतिकृतः - the I-thought creates; : भेदः - divisions; भयं - fear; च - and; बलिराजा इव - like King Bali; परमेश्वरस्य - to the Lord; प्रीत्या - with love; अहन्ता-ममता - (one's) ego and my-ness; समर्पणम् - to offer; भक्तिः - (is called) bhakti; मृत्युभयम् - the fear of death; सर्वप्रसिद्धम् - is well known to all; स्वरसवाही विदुषःअपि - even in knowledgeable persons (as in others); तथारूढो-अभिनिवेशः - fear of death is natural and present; तथा -also; श्री रमणेन प्रोक्तम् - is said by Śrī Ramana; मृत्युञ्जयम् - the conquerer of death; मृत्युभियाश्रितानाम् - for those, who in fear of death take refuge in the Lord; अहं मतिः - the I-thought ; मृत्युं - ends (itself); उपैति - gains; पूर्वम् - quickly; तत्र - thereafter; को मोहः - how can there be delusion; कः शोकः - how can there be sorrow; किं भयम् - how can there be fear; एकत्वं अनुपश्यतः - for the one who has seen the one Self in all?

Now I shall describe Bhakti Yoga – the Path of Devotion. The I-thought creates all divisions and fears. To offer with love one's ego and my-ness to the Lord, like King Bali, is called devotion. The fear of death is well known to all. Abhiniveśa – fear of death is natural and present even in knowledgeable persons as in others. Śrī Ramaṇa has said,

'For those, who in fear of death take refuge in the Lord, who is the conquerer of death, the I-thought itself ends.' Thereafter how can there be delusion or sorrow? Where is fear for one who has seen the one Self in all?

Jñāna and Bhakti: In the Path of Knowledge, the mind is made subtle by contemplation and inquiry and the ego is falsified (bādhita-ahaṅkāra) in the Realisation of the infinite Truth/Self. In devotion, the mind gets purified with the love of God and the ego is surrendered at the feet of the Lord.

Bhakti Yoga: Devotion is supreme love for the Supreme Lord. In the love of the Lord, one loves all, as the Lord is all. For the devotee, the Lord is his all-in-all. We lovingly, willingly and happily give when we love someone. We see an otherwise egoistic father, happily brought to his knees by his three year old who wants to make his papa a horse. The devotee surrenders his all – possessions, relations, body, actions and thoughts and finally surrenders himself to the Lord.

It is the 'I thought' alone that creates the duality of me versus the world, me and mine, you and yours. This differentiation creates alienation and fear which creates further alienation. In the deep sleep there is no 'I thought' and therefore no duality, alienation or fear.

The Lord Vāmana, as a young brāhmaṇa, asked King Bali for three feet of land. With one foot He covered the entire earth and with the second, the three worlds. Left with nothing to call his own, King Bali with love, offered his own head (ego) to the Lord, who made him immortal.

Fear of death is the most deeply rooted and instinctive fear seen in all of us. We never want our existence to end. Those who commit suicide only wish to put an end to their sorrow and not their existence. Bhagavān Ramana Maharshi recommends the Path of Devotion for those who are scared, especially of death. He advises them to surrender their ego at the feet of the immortal Lord. When the ego is destroyed, the devotee merges with the Lord and realises his own immortal nature. Where is the chance for fear in one who is immortal?

Śrī Kṛṣṇa urges Arjuna also to leave all cares and surrender to Him[1], and when Arjuna does so, his

[1] *sarvadharmān-parityajya mām-ekaṁ śaraṇaṁ vraja – Gītā* 18.66

confusions, sorrows and fears are destroyed. He picks up his abandoned bow, fights the battle and wins.

A great Master saw a seeker approaching him from afar and said, 'Drop'. The seeker dropped the fruits he was carrying. He again said, 'Drop'. The seeker paused for a second, prostrated and went away. The Master explained how that seeker had realised the Truth. The fruits represented his possessions and the accumulated fruits of actions which he first surrendered. Thereafter he surrendered his ego which owns and disowns everything. Having given up his finite ego (I-ness) and possessions (my-ness), he realised the Truth, prostrated with gratitude and left.

3 Relative Fearlessness – Practical Means

At the transactional level we find ourselves plagued with various fears. The Lord now gives us practical ways of dealing with them.

अथ व्यावहारदृष्ट्या भयनिवारणोपायाः । भयकारणानि अनेकानि । रागात् भयम् । रागस्य मूलं देहासक्तिः । आसक्तिवशात् सुखाभासोऽपि दुःखयोनिरेव । भोगे रोगभयं कुले च्युतिभयं वित्ते नृपालात् भयम् इत्यादि प्रसिद्धम् । वैराग्यमेव अभयम् ॥

तस्मात् वीतरागी भव । सत्सङ्गत्वे निस्सङ्गत्वं स्यात् तथैव इन्द्रियसंयमात् कर्मयोगाच्च ॥

atha vyāvahāra-dṛṣṭyā bhaya-nivāraṇopāyāḥ, bhaya-kāraṇāni anekāni, rāgāt bhayam, rāgasya mūlaṁ dehāsaktiḥ, āsaktivaśāt sukhābhāso'pi duḥkha-yonir-eva, bhoge roga-bhayaṁ kule cyuti-bhayaṁ vitte nṛpālāt bhayam ityādi prasiddham, vairāgyam-eva abhayam.

tasmāt vītarāgī bhava, satsaṅgatve nissaṅgatvaṁ syāt tathaiva indriya-saṁyamāt karma-yogācca.

अथ - now (we shall discuss); व्यावहारदृष्ट्या - from the practical standpoint; भयनिवारणोपायाः - the ways of removing fear; भयकारणानि - the causes of fear; अनेकानि - are countless; रागात् भयम् - fear is caused due to attachment; रागस्य मूलम् - The root (cause) of attachment; देहासक्तिः - attachment to the body; आसक्तिवशात् - due to attachment; सुखाभासः - the apparent joy; अपि - too; दुःखयोनिः - becomes the cause for sorrow; भोगे - (attachment) to pleasures; रोगभयम् - (causes) fear of diseases; कुले - (attachment) to family lineage; च्युतिभयम् - fear of fall; वित्ते - (attachment) to wealth; नृपालात्भयम् - fear of the king (government or tax office); इत्यादि - and so on; प्रसिद्धम् - is well known; वैराग्यम् - detachment; एव - alone; अभयम् - (makes one) fearless

तस्मात् - therefore; वीतरागी - detached; भव - become; सत्सङ्गत्वे - by keeping the company of noble people; निःसङ्गत्वम् - one becomes; स्यात् - and; तथैव - also; इन्द्रियसंयमात् - by controlling the senses; कर्मयोगाच्च - by Karma Yoga

Now we shall discuss the ways of removing fear from the practical standpoint. The causes of fear are countless. One should remove them by adopting appropriate means. Fear is caused due to attachment. All attachments arise out of the

attachment to the body. Due to attachment, the apparent joy too becomes the cause for sorrow. It is well known that attachment to pleasure causes fear of diseases, attachment to family lineage causes fear of fall; attachment to wealth causes fear of the king (government or tax office) and so on. Detachment alone makes one fearless.

Therefore become detached. By keeping the company of noble people, one becomes detached, and also by controlling the senses or by practising Karma Yoga.

Each of us has our pet fears which we nurture and nourish. Here we are advised to put forth efforts to get rid of them by appropriate means, as they harm and result in sorrow.

1. **Attachments cause fear:** When we superimpose happiness on things and people we fall for them and then get attached to them. The more they seem joy-giving the more we are attached and the more the expectations and finally more disappointments, and sorrow. The more the attachment, the greater is the fear of losing the object, person, name, fame, power or comforts. If we look at our lives, we find that the one we love the most, is always the cause for the greatest sorrow and for whom we fear the most.

Love is all about giving, forgiving, adjusting, understanding and accepting. But when love takes the form of attachment, it becomes demanding, possessive, jealous, expecting, insisting and controlling. It naturally becomes the cause of sorrow and fear.

Attachment to pleasures and comforts causes fear of losing them. Indulgence gives rise to the fear of disease (bhoge roga bhayam). We know well that smoking leads to lung cancer, heavy drinking to liver sclerosis, over-eating to obesity and compulsive social networking to social incompatibility.

A person attached to name fears infamy. The rich are haunted by many fears – of taxes, thieves, selfish relations and even their own children.[1] Indeed detachment alone makes us fearless and happy.[2]

However we should understand that the root of attachment to others is the attachment to our own body, as all relations with others are only on the basis of the body. Without detaching from our own body and our mind, detachment with others will be

[1] *putrādapi dhana-bhājāṁ bhītiḥ – Bhaja Govindam* 29
[2] *kasya sukhaṁ na karoti virāgaḥ – Bhaja Govindam* 18

temporary and we will only replace one object of attachment with another.

So how should we develop detachment? A few ways are indicated.

a. **Attachment-detachment:** When we attach ourselves to the higher, we can detach from the lower. Devāsakti (attachment to God) will help us remove dehāsakti (attachment to the body). But how does one get attached to God? Through the company of noble souls, we learn of God and His glories and learn to love Him. Also attachment to the noble souls, helps us overcome attachment to worldly souls[1] which is finally removed through attachment with God.

b. **Self-control:** An indulgent life style will only increase our attachments. The fires of desires and passions cannot be reduced when they are constantly fuelled by indulgence. Simple living and high thinking and exercising self-control will reduce our attachment to the body and to others.

[1] *sarva-saṅgadoṣaharā hi te – Bhāgavatam 3.25.24*

c. **Karma Yoga:** Detachment is to be free of both likes and dislikes. One who hates the world is as dependent on the world as one who is attached to things and beings. When we choicelessly perform our duties and are engaged in noble deeds, working without ego and selfishness with love and dedication for a higher cause or God, we are able to overcome our likes and dislikes and gain detachment. When actions become an offering to Him, the results become a gift from Him.

*****

भाविचिन्तनात् भयम्। सत्कार्ये अभिप्रवृत्तो भव।
स्वसत्कर्माणि प्रवृत्तस्य चिन्ताराहित्यं समयाभावात्॥

bhāvicintanāt bhayam, satkārye abhipravṛtto bhava,
svasatkarmāṇi pravṛttasya cintārāhityaṁ samayābhāvāt.

भाविचिन्तनात् - from worrying about the future; भयम् - fear (arises); सत्कार्ये - in good actions; अभिप्रवृत्तो - occupied in; भव - be (remain); स्वसत्कर्माणि प्रवृत्तस्य -of the one who is occupied with good action; चिन्ताराहित्यं - absence of worrying; समयाभावात् - due to non-availability of time.

Fear arises from worrying about the future. Remain occupied in good actions. One will have no time for worrying and will become free of fear arising thereby.

2. **Worries and fears:** Impractical expectations and negative imaginations about the future cause worries. We also have a fear of change and a fear of the unknown which add to our anxiety. Thoughts like, 'what will happen, I hope it does not happen, but I think it will happen, what if it happens ...' preoccupy a worried person. Some habitual worriers even worry that they have nothing to worry about! Some have got into this habit from childhood and have never felt the need to get out of this wrong thinking pattern.

'Sorry! No worry': This was a sign put by a husband whose wife was a chronic worrier. Worry is futile. It saps our mental energy, wastes our precious present, clutters our mind with unproductive thoughts and dullens our intellect. It can also give us peptic ulcers! Mark Twain said, 'There were lots of problems in my life. Some of them actually happened.'

Accepting the worst case scenario, helps us dismiss all other imagined consequences in between. A newly married girl was always scared of what her husband would do, as he ended many of his instructions with 'or else ...' A few months later, he told her, "Five of my friends are coming. You had better get dinner ready in a couple of hours, or else ..." Advised by her friend, she put her hands on her hips and said, "Or else what?" He meekly said, "Or else, I will cook the meal myself!"

Thoughts like 'What if I die, what if I get old' must be countered with accepting the inevitability of death and old age.[1] Someone joked that there was no use worrying about life because nobody gets out alive! We must learn to accept what comes to us in the present. The future too will come to us as the present and we must learn to accept whatever comes, when it comes. 'Que sera sera, whatever will be will be, the future's not ours to see, que sera sera, what will be will be.'

A good way to get rid of worries is to keep ourselves occupied in the performance of our duties and in creative and noble deeds. Our mind will remain focussed in the present and we shall have no time to worry. For those with faith in God, it would be good to leave all worries on Him. Śrī Gurudev

[1] *tasmād-aparihārye'rthe na tvaṁ śocitum-arhasi – Gītā* 2.27

advised, 'You do your best and leave the rest to Him.' One devotee told God, 'Be my partner in work. I will do the work, You do the worrying!'

*****

एकान्तवासे अन्यभूतेभ्यः सर्पचोरादिभयम् ।
एकान्तशीलो भव । अहिंसा-दया-प्रेमादि-विवर्धने
अभयत्वम् ॥

ekāntavāse anyabhūtebhyaḥ sarpa-corādibhayam,
ekāntaśīlo bhava, ahiṁsā-dayā-premādi-vivardhane
abhayatvam.

एकान्तवासे - in a solitary place; अन्यभूतेभ्यः - of other beings; सर्पचोरादि - snakes, thieves and so on; भयम् - (there is) fear; एकान्तशीलो भव - keep going to such places; अहिंसा - non-injury; दया - compassion; प्रेमादि - love and so on; विवर्धने - (when they) increase; अभयत्वम् - one becomes fearless

In a solitary place there is fear of other beings like snakes, thieves and so on. Keep going to such places. When the qualities like non-injury, compassion and love increase one becomes fearless even in solitary places.

3. **Fear of solitude:** We are scared of being alone – actually scared of others when we are alone. Some do not like to be alone. If we do not like our own company, how will others like it!

People are scared of frogs, lizards, cockroaches, dogs or cats. Many more are scared of snakes and scorpions, which they are likely to encounter in nature. And all of us would be scared of lions, wild elephants or tigers which we may encounter in forests. Animals and such creatures always behave according to their nature. If we know that, we learn how to deal with them. When we stay in solitude, we learn to live in harmony with all creatures and our fear disappears. One saint described how in peak winters in Gangotri, he would shake out his blanket in the morning as one or two scorpions would have taken shelter in its warmth at night!

People are scared to be alone because other people like thieves could harm them. We should take necessary precautions, and thereafter leave all care to God. Seeing that Swami Tapovanam had nothing, some thieves who came to loot him gave him food and a blanket.

*****

घोरविक्षिप्तादिस्वदोषान् निरीक्ष्य स्ववृत्तिभ्यः भयम्। प्रकृतेः गुणेभ्यः वृत्तयः उद्भवन्ति। तान् अप्रतिकारपूर्वकं साक्षिभावेन ईक्षस्व। अनित्यत्वात् नश्याः॥

ghora-vikṣiptādi-svadoṣān nirīkṣya svavṛttibhyaḥ bhayam, prakṛteḥ guṇebhyaḥ vṛttayaḥ udbhavanti, tān apratikārapūrvakaṁ sākṣi-bhāvena īkṣasva, anityatvāt naśyāḥ.

घोर-विक्षिप्तादि-स्वदोषान् निरीक्ष्य - seeing one's own terrible and agitated thoughts and faults; स्ववृत्तिभ्यः - from ones own thoughts; भयम् - one gets scared; प्रकृतेः गुणेभ्यः - due to our nature; वृत्तयः - thoughts; उद्भवन्ति - arise; तान् - them; अप्रतिकारपूर्वकं - without reaction; साक्षिभावेन - as a witness; ईक्षस्व - observe; अनित्यत्वात् - (being) fleeting by (nature); नश्याः - they will end (on their own)

One gets scared of one's own terrible and agitated thoughts and faults. Thoughts arise due to our nature. Observe them as a witness. Being fleeting by nature, they will end on their own.

4. **Fear of our own thoughts:** Many are persecuted by their own thoughts. Compulsive, obsessive, negative, criminal or worrying thoughts or hatred,

anger, passion and such strong emotions overwhelm us. Many escape from their thoughts through drinks and drugs, some through indulgence and work. However, troubled thoughts keep coming back. Some are even driven to psychotic and delusory thinking or get depressed and need medication to dullen their thoughts. Unfortunately many of us think too much but do not act enough. We have never learnt how to think and so we get into wrong patterns of thinking. Creative activity, performance of duties, spiritual practices like yoga, pūjā, japa and meditation, regular and appropriate eating, sleeping and entertainment would help us control our thoughts. Practice of the attitude of being a witness definitely helps to purge unwanted thoughts and tendencies.

*****

निर्बलेषु भयं दृश्यते विशेषतो स्त्रीषु । बलिष्ठा भव । स्वरक्षोपायेन मनोबलेन प्रपत्त्या वा । नायमात्मा बलहीनेन लभ्यः । निर्बलत्वं लोकेष्वपि निन्द्यम् ॥

nirbaleṣu bhayaṁ dṛśyate viśeṣato strīṣu, baliṣṭhā bhava, svarakṣopāyena manobalena prapattyā vā, nāyamātmā balahīnena labhyaḥ, nirbalatvaṁ lokeṣvapi nindyam.

निर्बलेषु - among weak people; भयम् - fear; दृश्यते - is seen; विशेषतः - especially; स्त्रीषु - in women; बलिष्ठा भव - be brave; स्वरक्षोपायेन - with method(s) of self-defence; मनोबलेन - with will power; प्रपत्त्या वा - (or) surrendering (to a higher altar); अयमात्मा - this Self; बलहीनेन - by the weak; न - is not ; लभ्यः - gained (realised) ; निर्बलत्वम् - weakness; लोकेष्वपि - even in the world; निन्द्यम् - is not respected

A weak person is fearful, especially women. Be brave and daring by equipping oneself with methods of self-defence, willpower or surrendering to a higher altar. Self-realisation is not gained by the weak. Weakness is not respected anywhere in the world.

5. **The weak are fearful:** It is seen that those who are physically and mentally weak are always scared of being hurt by others. We find more people physically and mentally weak than ever before. Medicine has advanced but health has deteriorated. In many societies weak children grow up to become weak parents who in turn raise weak children.

In this world only the fit survive so we have to make ourselves physically and mentally strong.

Lokmanya Tilak took a year off from his studies to make his sick body strong. Thereafter he pioneered the freedom movement of India and was put through much physical and mental trouble which he faced courageously. When the going gets tough, only the tough keep going.

We must empower ourselves with courage to face life's challenges, strength of character to overcome temptations, guts to be adventurous, patience and forbearance to go through tough times and a sense of humour to laugh through life.

Most societies are male dominant. Women therefore need the extra strength to protect themselves and become successful. Most women inherently have qualities which are her strengths like feminity, sensitivity, multitasking, communication skills (termed talkative by men) ... and many more. So instead of trying to be manly or competitive she should be comfortable and happy, being a woman and capitalise on her strengths. She should stand up for her own rights and stand up also against the wrongs done towards herself and other women. Unity is strength and a united women force can remove many evils against women and fears from their minds.

*****

दारिद्र्ये भयम्। कर्मरतो भव।
निजकर्मोपात्तेन वित्तेन विनोदय चित्तम्॥

dāridrye bhayam, karmarato bhava,
nijakarmopāttena vittena vinodaya cittam.

दारिद्र्ये भयम् - poverty causes fear; कर्मरतो भव - work hard; निजकर्मोपात्तेन वित्तेन - by the wealth earned through one's self-effort.; विनोदय - enjoy; चित्तम् - yourself

Poverty causes fear. Work hard. Enjoy yourself by the wealth earned through one's self-effort.

6. **Poverty causes fear:** Food, clothing and shelter are the basic necessities of life. Some do not have to worry about these. But many are uncertain even about their next meal and that naturally causes anxiety. To lose a job is a tragedy for one whose family is living hand to mouth. Education and hard work can bring us out of such a condition.

Unfortunately in India lucrative self-employment opportunities are not taken up and majority join the line for employment as engineers, doctors and IT graduates. Professions chosen according to our inherent abilities, give us a lifetime of satisfaction and success and removes many causes for tension and anxiety.[1]

*****

Lord Śiva concludes this teaching with -

एवं विविधा भयानि लोके दृश्यन्ते । तानि सर्वाणि द्वैताश्रयाणि । स्वरूपज्ञानेन अद्वैतपदम् । तेन अभयम् । नान्यः पन्था अभयाय विद्यते । ये उपायाः निरूपिताः तान् स्वयं पुनः धिया विचार्य तेषु प्रतिष्ठिता भव । तेन सुखी भव । शिवमस्तु ॥

evaṁ vividhā bhayāni loke dṛśyante, tāni sarvāṇi dvaitāśrayāṇi, svarūpa-jñānena advaitapadam, tena abhayam, nānyaḥ panthā abhayāya vidyate, ye upāyāḥ nirūpitāḥ tān svayaṁ punaḥ dhiyā vicārya teṣu pratiṣṭhitā bhava, tena sukhī bhava, śivamastu.

एवं - thus; विविधा - many forms; भयानि - (of) fear; लोके - in the world; दृश्यन्ते - are seen; तानि सर्वाणि - all of them; द्वैताश्रयाणि - (are caused) due to the notion of duality; स्वरूपज्ञानेन - by Self-knowledge; अद्वैतपदम् -

[1] *sve sve karmaṇyabhirataḥ saṁsiddhiṁ labhate naraḥ* – *Gītā* 18.45; *paradharmo bhayāvahaḥ* – *Gītā* 3.35

(one attains) the non-dual state; तेन अभयम् - by which one becomes fearless; नान्यः पन्था - no other path; अभयाय - to (total) fearlessness; विद्यते - there is; ये उपायाः - these means; निरूपिताः - that have been described; तान् - them; पुनः - again; धिया - with intelligence; विचार्य - having thought; तेषु - in them; प्रतिष्ठिता भव - be steadfast (in) following; तेन - by that; सुखीभव - be happy; शिवमस्तु - may you gain auspiciousness

Thus there are many forms of fear seen in the world. All are caused due to the notion of duality. By Self-knowledge one attains the non-dual state by which one becomes fearless. There is no other path to (total) fearlessness. Reflect intelligently on these means that I have described again. Be steadfast in following the same. May you be happy. May you gain auspiciousness.

7. **Many more fears:** Each of us has many more fears. Some are troubled by various phobias like fear of heights and fear of closed places. These are caused due to an incident in the present or the past life. People have got cured by going to their root, some even through regression into the past life.

Fear of failure is also common. Did we not fall a hundred times before we learnt to walk? We never made a prestige issue of falling and so we are now walking easily. A scientist said, 'I discovered a hundred ways of not doing the experiment. Based on that, the scientist who tried the 101st way, succeeded in getting the result.' Try, try and we succeed.

Most people are scared of public speaking. They get tongue-tied at the thought of becoming the laughing stock for all. A speaker asked a chef how he cooked such excellent food each day. He replied, 'The same way you give excellent speeches each day!' Each have overcome their initial fear, practised and perfected their skill and love what they do.

The list of fears is endless and there are practical means to overcome them also. However, the only permanent solution to fear is to be established in our true infinite, non-dual nature, which is fearless and immortal.

4 Epilogue

तदा सा साधिका विमलबोधेन आनन्दमग्ना सन् प्रेमाश्रुधारया शिवम् अभिषिञ्च्य मनसा पूजयित्वा पुनः पुनर्नमस्कृत्य प्रार्थितवती च - भो शिव भवद्भक्तिमेव स्थिरां देहि मह्यम्। हे कृपाशील शम्भो कृतार्थोऽस्मि तस्मात्॥

तदनन्तरम् अन्तः स्थितं सत्यं शिवं सुन्दरं शान्तम् अद्वैतम् अभयं ध्यात्वा किञ्चित् कालं तद्भावं गता। भुजङ्गोऽपि निर्भयेन बहिर्गतः॥

tadā sā sādhikā vimala-bodhena ānandamagnā san premāśru-dhārayā śivam abhiṣiñcya manasā pūjayitvā punaḥ punar-namaskṛtya prārthitavatī ca – bho śiva bhavad-bhaktim-eva sthirāṁ dehi mahyam. he kṛpāśīla śambho kṛtārtho'smi tasmāt.

tadanantaram antaḥ sthitaṁ satyaṁ śivaṁ sundaraṁ śāntam advaitam abhayaṁ dhyātvā kiñcit kālaṁ tadbhāvaṁ gatā, bhujaṅgo'pi nirbhayena bahirgataḥ.

तदा - thereafter; सा साधिका - that seeker; विमलबोधेन - by this pure Knowledge; आनन्दमग्ना सन् - being immersed in joy; प्रेमाश्रुधारया - with tears of love overflowing; शिवम् अभिषिञ्च्य - giving bath to Śiva; मनसा पूजयित्वा - worshipping mentally; पुनः पुनः नमस्कृत्य - prostrating again and again; प्रार्थितवती - prayed thus; च - and; भो शिव - O Śiva; भवद्भक्तिमेव - devotion for You only; स्थिराम् - steady; देहि - give; मह्यम् -to me; हे कृपाशील - O compassionate; शम्भो - Śambhu; कृतार्थोऽस्मि - I am fulfilled; तस्मात् - by it

तदनन्तरम् - thereafter; अन्तः स्थितम् - residing within; सत्यम् - Truth; शिवम् - auspiciousness; सुन्दरम् - beauty; शान्तम् - peaceful; अद्वैतम् - non-dual; अभयम् - fearless; ध्यात्वा - having meditated; किञ्चित् कालम् - for a while; तद्भावम् गता - she was in that state (of meditation); भुजङ्गः - snake; अपि - even; निर्भयेन - fearlessly; बहिर्गतः - went away

Thereafter that seeker, immersed in this rare Knowledge, with tears of love overflowing for the Lord and mentally worshipping and prostrating again and again, prayed thus, 'Oh Śambhu, may there be steady devotion for You in me, Oh compassionate Śambhu, may I be fulfilled by it.'

Thereafter, being (in a state of meditation) on the Lord residing within as Truth, Auspiciousness, Beauty, Peace, non-dual, fearlessness, time passed by for a while. The snake too went away fearlessly.

This knowledge given by Lord Śiva out of compassion to this blessed soul filled her with deep love and gratitude. Tears of love and joy flowed freely and she mentally worshipped the Lord of her heart. In sheer gratitude she prostrated again and again and prayed to the Lord. 'Please do always shower Your grace on me, fill my heart with abiding and unswerving devotion and fulfil me with the realisation of my own infinite nature.' Her mind became still and she remained in divine contemplation for some time. When she opened her eyes, she saw that the snake had gone away as had the fear in her.

This is the end of a seeker's story written for my own reflection in the form of *Abhaya Vidyā*. I pray that this knowledge helps us also to face fear. May peace, beauty, auspiciousness and fearlessness prevail.

॥ॐ तत्सत् शिवार्पणमस्तु ॥

om tat sat śivārpaṇamastu

Notes